Biff, Chip and Kipper went to have
dinner with Lee's family.

"This is a special meal," said Lee. "It's
New Year's Eve!"

"But New Year's Eve was weeks ago,"
said Biff.

"Chinese New Year is on a different day,"
said Grandpa Chen.

√Lee and Lin were wearing red tops.

"It is a tradition to wear red for the New Year," said Lee.

"In our family we always have fish for dinner at Chinese New Year," said Mum.

"And we have these little dumplings!" said Lin.

At dinner, Chip asked Grandpa about
Chinese New Year.

"Each year is named after an animal.
There are twelve animals in all," said Grandpa.

"Tell them the story about the animals, Grandpa!" cried Lin.

Grandpa began the story. "A long time ago in China, there were lots of animals."

"There were tigers and dogs, monkeys
and horses," he said. "There were rabbits
and snakes, and even dragons."

"The Emperor wanted to name each year
after a different animal," said Grandpa.
"Which animal was going to be first?"

"The Emperor decided to hold a race
for all the animals. The first year would be
named after the winner."

"I think the tiger won the race," said
Chip. "They're very fast."

"Rabbits are really quick, too," said Biff.

√"I bet the dragon won!" said Kipper.
"Dragons can fly! They would easily beat
all the other animals!"

Lee just shook his head. "Nobody has picked the right animal yet," he said.

"Tell them about the river, Grandpa," said Lin.

Grandpa went on. "The big day came. The animals had to race across a wide river."

"A river?" said Chip. "I wonder which of the animals was the best swimmer."

"Some snakes can swim well," said Biff.

"In fact, Ox was the strongest swimmer,"
said Grandpa. "He was soon in the lead."

"Ox didn't know Rat and Cat had hopped onto his back," said Grandpa. "They planned to jump when Ox came close to the riverbank."

"I bet Cat won," said Biff. "Cats can jump much further than rats."

"Tell them, Grandpa," said Lin.

Just then there was a noise from outside.
It was a cat.

"Wait a moment," said Grandpa. "It is
time for *my* new year tradition."

Grandpa Chen put some fish on a plate.
He opened the back door and called to
the cat.

"What about the story?" asked Chip.
"Who won?"

"Rat did!" said Lee. "Cat slipped and fell
in the water!"

"By the time Cat finished the race, everybody had left. Now there would be no Year of the Cat. Cat was angry, especially with Rat."

"So why do you feed that cat?" Kipper
asked Grandpa.

"I was born in the Year of the Rat," said
Grandpa.

"At the start of the New Year I like to feed
that cat to say sorry for the race!"

The cat walked away with its tail in the air.

"But look," said Grandpa. "Even now cats don't like rats!"